Songs and chants for first steps in ...

SINGING PHONICS

Helen MacGregor
Catherine Birt

BOOK 1

Bam
Bim

rrrrrroar

sssplasshh

A&CB

A & C BLACK MUSIC

AN IMPRINT OF BLOOMSBURY

LONDON   NEW DELHI   NEW YORK   SYDNEY

CONTENTS

ASPECT 1 – SOUNDS AROUND
Environmental sounds

ASPECT 2 – PLAY SOUNDS
Instrumental sounds

ASPECT 3 – BODY SOUNDS
Body percussion

ASPECT 4 – TIME TO RHYME
Rhythm and rhyme

ASPECT 5 – SOUNDS THE SAME
Alliteration

ASPECT 6 – SINGING SOUNDS
Voice Sounds

ASPECT 7 – SOUND TALK
Oral blending and segmenting

First published 2008
by A&C Black Publishers Ltd
An imprint of Bloomsbury Publishing Plc
50 Bedford Square, London, WC1B 3DP.
Reprinted 2010, 2012.

Copyright © Helen MacGregor, Catherine Birt
and Steve Grocott 2008
CD – A&C Black 2008

ISBN 978-1-4081-0472-9

Edited by Laura White
Designed by Fi Grant
Cover illustration © Sandsra Isaaksson 2008
Inside illustrations © Emily Skinner 2008
CD produced by Steve Grocott 2008
Performed by Kaz Simmons and Cleveland Watkiss
Music set by David Weston
Printed by Martins the Printers, Berwick-upon-Tweed

A&C Black uses paper produced with elemental chlorine-free pulp, harvested from managed sustainable forests.

INTRODUCTION

Singing Phonics 1 is a songbook bursting with stimulating, interactive and imaginative play-based activities designed to motivate and support the teaching of phonics in Foundation Stage and Key Stage 1.

The songs exemplify good practice in phonics teaching for each of the seven aspects at Phase 1 as set out in the **Letters and Sounds** DfE programme. Each chapter in this songbook represents one of the seven aspects in the document.

Chidren explore a wide range of sounds both aurally and orally, and become more confident at using their own voices. These fundamental requirements lay the foundations for further phonemic awareness and later systematic phonics work with young children.

The Singing Phonics songs

Most of the songs in **Singing Phonics 1** are traditional melodies written with new lyrics to enhance phonic work. There are also new chants and songs with original melodies in the book. The melody lines for all songs are on pages 70 to 78.

 CD track number Flash cards

Links to the Letters and Sounds document

The main strand of each set of activities is divided into three areas of learning. Each area is indicated by an icon and a **Letters and Sounds** key (at the bottom of each activity page) which links to the curriculum.

Tuning into sounds (auditory discrimination).

Listening and remembering (auditory memory and sequencing).

Talking about sounds (developing vocabulary and language comprehension).

Sounds around Aspect 1 – General sound discrimination – environmental sounds. Encouraging the children to listen, recognise and discriminate between sounds in the environment.

Play sounds Aspect 2 – General sound discrimination – instrumental sounds. It is recommended that young children explore and develop awareness and confidence in using their own voice and body to produce sounds before introducing the use of instruments.

Body sounds Aspect 3 – General sounds discrimination – body percussion. Developing movement, awareness of the body and co-ordinating skills is an important support for phonics work.

Time to rhyme Aspect 4 – Rhythm and rhyme. Young children need to experience rhyme in order to develop an understanding of the sounds of words and syllables.

Sounds the same Aspect 5 – Alliteration. The children develop recognition of words which start with the same sound.

Singing sounds Aspect 6 – Voice sounds. Exploring sounds made with the voice and learning how to control the child's own instrument.

Sound talk Aspect 7 – Oral blending and segmenting Oral segmenting and blending is the sounding and joining of phonemes to create words, eg, h-a-t said together is hat.

SINGING PHONICS 1 © HELEN MACGREGOR & CATHERINE BIRT 2008 A & C BLACK PUBLISHERS LTD

About the activities
Using the song

The songs and activities in **Singing Phonics 1** can be and should be used in different ways.

Songs for listening

– use the CD to encourage the children to join in with the vocal sounds only or repeating patterns at the appropriate places (eg whirr, whirr etc in Professor Brain's Amazing Machine, Pg 56).

Songs for games

– the practitioner should learn the songs and use them independently of the CD, adapting and extending them with props, words, sounds or phonemes of their own choice to suit the needs of the class (eg, Copycats, Pg 32).

Songs children to sing

– encourage the children to learn by singing along with the CD and with you so that they can sing the songs independently during child-initiated play (eg Squeaky door, Pg 14).

Child-initiated play

Use these ideas for indoor and outdoor play. The activities encourage the children to learn through play by exploring, consolidating and developing the concepts introduced in the songs.

Extend the activities

Once the children are confident with the songs and have completed their own tasks there are ideas to help the practitioner develop the games further. These are suggestions which will challenge the children who are ready to progress to more demanding activities.

The CD

Each of the songs in **Singing Phonics 1** has a lively, fun track. See full track listings at the front of the book. The CD icon at the top of each activity gives the track number (see key, Pg 4).

Resources

The 'What you will need' box lists any resources which are needed for an activity.

A selection of picture and letter cards are included on Pgs 79–80 which can be used for several of the activities.

Practitioners may photocopy any illustration as many times as is necessary and create picture cards. There is a list of illustrations at the back of the book.

About phonics

Research has shown that effective teaching of phonics is through multi-sensory, interactive and fun ways across all areas of learning and play.

A phoneme is the smallest unit of sound in a word made by one or more letters, for instance, *sh* in sheep or *ee* in deep.

Oral segmenting and blending

Aspect 7 of **Letters and Sounds** and chapter 7 of **Singing Phonics 1** (Sound talk) develops oral segmenting and blending. This chapter should not be attempted until the children are confident with all other Aspects (1–6). These activities should only be used when children are ready to hear a series of separate sounds (phonemes) in a word, segment and then merge them back together to make the spoken world blend, eg, h-a-t makes 'hat'.

Oral segmenting – to hear phonemes in a word and sound talk them, eg, h-a-t.

Oral blending – to merge the separate phonemes back together to say the whole word, eg, 'hat.'

How to sound talk

Correct enunciation of phonemes is vital. The phoneme at the beginning of 'mat' for example should be said 'mmmm' not 'muh'.

The phonemes for p, c, t need to be articulated without voice (almost a whisper) and not 'puh', 'cuh' and 'tuh'. Adding the 'uh' sound causes confusion when children begin to spell and write. For correct enunciation see the DVD included in **Letters and Sounds** documents Ref: DCSF 00281-2007BKT-EN.

SOUNDS AROUND

Using the song

🔊 Listen to track 1.

Discuss each of the sounds the children noticed in the song and experiment making vocal sounds for each verse to represent rain, wind and sea, eg, rain – sssss; wind – hoooo; sea – whoosh.

Play the song again, encouraging the children to join in with the chosen vocal sounds in the appropriate places.

Child-initiated play

☺ Place pictures of environmental sound sources where the children can use them to explore making the sounds with their voices, eg, dripping tap, traffic.

Prompt them to explore sounds with other themes using toys, pictures or percussion instruments as a stimulus, eg, minibeasts, animals, transport, musical instruments.

Extend the activities

👂 Go on a listening walk to notice the sounds around.

Sing the chorus of the song together. Ask the children for a sound they can hear, eg, cars and then sing the verse with new words of your own, eg,

**Listen to the cars,
Oh, listen to the cars,**
(Everybody listens carefully)
Listen to the cars.

If possible, record the sounds you hear to take back and listen to later, or alternatively, take a photo or draw a picture of the sound source.

Recall the sounds you heard by singing the song with the children. Change the words as appropriate and play back the recording during line 3 of the verse, or sing matching vocal sounds suggested by the children, eg,

pebbles underfoot – crunch crunch
water swishing round – swish swish
bubbles in the air – bbbbbbb

Use the photos or pictures to remind the children of the list of sounds they collected.

What you will need

- Pictures or recordings of environmental sound sources, eg, rain, wind, sea.
- Other classroom stimuli, eg, toys, pictures, instruments.

LETTERS AND SOUNDS

FOCUS Aspect 1 – General sound discrimination (environmental sounds):
👂 Tuning into sounds (auditory discrimination)
🔊 Listening and remembering (auditory memory and sequencing)
☺ Talking about sounds (developing vocabulary and language comprehension)

SOUNDS AROUND
Tune: Farmer's in the den

Listen to the sounds,
Oh listen to the sounds.
All around us everywhere
Let's listen to the sounds.

Listen to the rain,
Oh listen to the rain.
(rain sounds)
Let's listen to the rain.

Listen to the sounds,
Oh listen to the sounds.
All around us everywhere
Let's listen to the sounds.

Listen to the wind,
Oh listen to the wind.
(wind sounds)
Let's listen to the wind.

Listen to the sounds,
Oh listen to the sounds.
All around us everywhere
Let's listen to the sounds.

Listen to the sea,
Oh listen to the sea.
(sea sounds)
Let's listen to the sea.

Listen to the sounds,
Oh listen to the sounds.
All around us everywhere
Let's listen to the sounds.

LISTENING BAG

Using the song

Prepare a cloth bag containing each of the objects mentioned in the song, then play track 2 to the children. Take out the matching object and show it to the children as you all listen to the sound it makes.

Child-initiated play

Now show the children how to play the game. Sit the children in a circle. Secretly place one of the objects in the bag and ask the children to pass the bag around the circle as you sing the first three lines. At the end of the third line of each verse, the child holding the bag removes the object and everyone names it. Complete the last line of the song and prompt the child to make the sound as everyone listens.

Discuss the sound you heard – was it quiet, loud, scrunchy, rattling? Can you think of a word to describe the sound, eg, jingle? Repeat the game with the objects suggested in the other verses.

Extend the activities

Play without the CD using other objects, eg, toys, animal picture cards.

Encourage the children to choose the sounds they think the object makes and use their own voices, eg,

> car: vroooom
>
> lorry: beep beep.

All copy the sound.

Change the second line to 'It's an instrument trying to hide.' to introduce a variety of percussion or instrument sounds (Aspect 2).

What you will need

- A cloth bag with a selection of objects which make a sound – keys, dried leaves, a paper bag, a twig, beach pebbles.

FOCUS Aspect 1 – General sound discrimination (environmental sounds):
- Tuning into sounds (auditory discrimination)
- Listening and remembering (auditory memory and sequencing)
- ☺ Talking about sounds (developing vocabulary and language comprehension)

LISTENING BAG
Tune: This old man

Listening bag, what's inside?
Something's in there trying to hide.
Put your hand in, see what you have found,
A bunch of keys, let's hear the sound. (jingle)

Listening bag, what's inside?
Something's in there, trying to hide.
Put your hand in, see what you have found,
Dried up leaves, let's hear the sound. (scrunch)

Listening bag, what's inside?
Something's in there, trying to hide.
Put your hand in, see what you have found,
A paper bag, let's hear the sound. (rustle)

Listening bag, what's inside?
Something's in there, trying to hide.
Put your hand in, see what you have found,
A snapping twig, let's hear the sound. (snap)

Listening bag, what's inside?
Something's in there, trying to hide.
Put your hand in, see what you have found,
Pebbles from the beach, let's hear the sound. (clunk)

THREE SMALL PETS

Using the song

Teach the song by asking the children to echo-sing the first two lines. As you sing the second line, reveal the pets and place them in a row where the children can all see.

Remove the last pet as indicated by the words, leaving two visible. Can the children make the missing sound of the third pet in the sequence? Reveal the pet to check their answer.

Child-initiated play

☺ Place the toy animals in other play areas, eg, sand tray, garden or outdoor area. Encourage the children to choose and arrange them then make new sequences of sounds with their voices. Can they play the 'missing game' with other children?

Extend the activities

Change the pets to explore other sounds and play the game again. You may like to change the first line, eg, three minibeasts, three little kids (use photos and children's names), three instruments (small percussion, eg, castanets, drum, shaker).

Make the game more challenging by removing the middle or the first sound. Can the children recall the sequence?

What you will need

- A collection of toy animals or laminated pictures, eg, cat, dog, mouse, bird, chicken, horse, snake, hamster, fish.

- Photocopies of Singing Phonics 1 illustrations can be used – see the list of illustrations at the back of the book.

LETTERS AND SOUNDS

FOCUS Aspect 1 – General sound discrimination (environmental sounds):
- Tuning into sounds (auditory discrimination)
- Listening and remembering (auditory memory and sequencing)
- ☺ Talking about sounds (developing vocabulary and language comprehension)

THREE SMALL PETS
Tune: Three blind mice

Three small pets,
Three small pets.
Meow woof squeak,
Meow woof squeak.
One of my pets is missing today.
Listen to this and can you say
Which of my pets has run away?
Meow woof ....

Three small pets,
Three small pets.
Meow woof squeak,
Meow woof squeak.
One of my pets is missing today.
Listen to this and can you say
Which of my pets has run away?
Meow .... squeak.

Three small pets,
Three small pets.
Meow woof squeak,
Meow woof squeak.
One of my pets is missing today.
Listen to this and can you say
Which of my pets has run away?
.... woof squeak.

HEAR, HEAR!

Using the song

🎧 Sing the song to the children (or join in with track 4), encouraging them to copy each of the sounds in the third line.

Once they are familiar with the song, sing it all the way through together.

Child-initiated play

🗨 Provide the children with 'small world' play props representing more environments to stimulate exploration of other sounds, eg, jungle with wild animals; house with people and furniture; machines.

Extend the activities

🎧 Can the children suggest different sounds for each verse, eg, cuckoo, cheep cheep? Confident individuals can make a sound for everyone to copy.

Combine two sounds to create a sequence, eg,

> In the city hear the cars.
>
> In the city hear the cars.
>
> Beep beep, vroom vroom.
>
> In the city hear the cars.

Visit different environments. Go on a listening walk and make up your own words for the song, eg, in the playground hear the bikes – ting ting; in the bathroom hear the taps – drip drip.

Provide dressing-up clothes and props for role-play and encourage the children to act out characters as they sing the song and make vocal sounds, eg, in the castle, hear the giant; in the forest, hear the bears.

What you will need

- A collection of 'small world' play props, representing environments, eg, jungle with animals, house with people and furniture, machines.

LETTERS AND SOUNDS

FOCUS Aspect 1 – General sound discrimination (environmental sounds):
🎧 Tuning into sounds (auditory discrimination)
🗨 Listening and remembering (auditory memory and sequencing)
☺ Talking about sounds (developing vocabulary and language comprehension)

HEAR, HEAR!
Tune: London's burning

In the kitchen, hear the clock.
In the kitchen, hear the clock.
Tick tock. (tick tock)
In the kitchen, hear the clock.

In the garden, hear the birds.
In the garden, hear the birds.
Tweet tweet. (tweet tweet)
In the garden, hear the birds.

In the playground, hear us play.
In the playground, hear us play.
Hooray! (Hooray!)
In the playground, hear us play.

At the seaside, hear the waves.
At the seaside, hear the waves.
Splish splash. (splish splash)
At the seaside, hear the waves.

In the jungle, hear the chimps.
In the jungle, hear the chimps.
Ooh ooh. (ooh ooh)
In the jungle, hear the chimps.

SQUEAKY DOOR

(5)

Using the song

🔊 Listen to the song (track 5).

Talk about possible actions to accompany the song. Listen to the song again or sing it yourself, encouraging the children to perform the suggested actions.

Encourage the children to join in with the singing and actions on different occasions until they are familiar with the song and can sing it without the CD.

Child-initiated play

☺ Encourage the children to perform actions whilst singing their own verses as they play indoors and outdoors.

Extend the activities

☺ Build up a sequence of sounds in line 4 of each verse, eg, splish splash splosh squeak, creak squeak.

Involve the children in helping to make up new verses by choosing other actions such as 'using bricks to build tall towers, tap, tap, tap' or 'swishing sand around the sand tray, swish, swish, swish'.

FOCUS Aspect 1 – General sound discrimination (environmental sounds):
🔊 Tuning into sounds (auditory discrimination)
🔊 Listening and remembering (auditory memory and sequencing)
☺ Talking about sounds (developing vocabulary and language comprehension)

SQUEAKY DOOR
Tune: In and out the dusty bluebells

Opening the squeaky door,
Opening the squeaky door,
Opening the squeaky door,
Squeak squeak squeak.

Jumping in the splashy puddles,
Jumping in the splashy puddles,
Jumping in the splashy puddles,
Splash splash splash.

Stamping on the crazy paving,
Stamping on the crazy paving,
Stamping on the crazy paving,
Stamp stamp stamp.

Listening in the gorgeous garden,
Listening in the gorgeous garden,
Listening in the gorgeous garden,
Buzz buzz buzz.

Running through the crunchy leaves,
Running through the crunchy leaves,
Running through the crunchy leaves,
Crunch crunch crunch.

Going in now we're all tired,
Going in now we're all tired,
Going in now we're all tired,
Yawn yawn yawn.

Last one close the squeaky door!
Last one close the squeaky door!
Last one close the squeaky door!
Shh shh shh.

I HEAR MUSIC

Using the song

🔊 Play track 6, asking the children to notice the instruments played in each verse.

Play the song again or sing it yourself, inviting the children to echo-sing the first two lines, then show them how to mime playing each instrument mentioned in the second half of each verse.

Play the song again. Encourage the children to mime playing the instruments mentioned, noticing when the instruments play and when they stop and matching with their movements.

Divide the children into four groups: shakers, drums, bells and cymbals, giving each child an instrument. Sing the song, inviting each group to make sounds freely on their instruments in the gaps in the song. They may need to try several times to control starting and stopping!

> ### What you will need
>
> • A selection of hand-held percussion instruments sufficient for all the children to have one each, eg, shakers, drums, bells, cymbals.

Child-initiated play

☺ Leave a selection of soundmakers and/or instruments outdoors or indoors where the children can explore making the sounds they have been introduced to through the song activities. Encourage the children by singing the song when you notice them making new sounds, eg,

> I hear music, I hear music,
>
> All around, all around.
>
> Listen to Nathan's tambourine
>
> Hear the sound.   Shake shake shake.

Extend the activities

🔊 Explore other instruments and soundmakers with the children to make up new verses and sounds, eg, listen to the wind chimes – tinkle tinkle tinkle; listen to the saucepan lid – tap tap tap.

Explore movement and body percussion sounds (Aspect 3) to make new verses of the song, eg, 'listen to the footsteps, clop clop clip'; 'listen to the knee knocks, knock knock knock'.

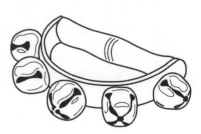

FOCUS Aspect 2 – General sound discrimination (instrumental sounds):
  🔊 Tuning into sounds (auditory discrimination)
  🔊 Listening and remembering (auditory memory and sequencing)
  ☺ Talking about sounds (developing vocabulary and language comprehension)

I HEAR MUSIC
Tune: Frère Jacques

I hear music, I hear music,
All around, all around.
Listen to the shakers.   (shaker plays)
Hear the sound.   Shake shake shake.

I hear music, I hear music,
All around, all around.
Listen to the drum beat.   (drum plays)
Hear the sound.   Boom boom boom.

I hear music, I hear music,
All around, all around.
Listen to the bells ring.   (bell rings)
Hear the sound.   Ting ting ting.

I hear music, I hear music,
All around, all around.
Listen to the cymbals.   (cymbal plays)
Hear the sound.   Swish swish swish.

READY, STEADY, STOP!

Using the song

🎧 Listen to the song before you play it to the children. Notice how each verse is sung differently depending on the lyrics, eg, 'Everyone play quietly' is sung quietly.

Demonstrate using the instruments as you sing the song. Encourage everyone to join in with the playing. The children should follow the instructions in each verse and hold their instrument still each time they hear 'stop!'

Play several times until the children are familiar with the game, then play track 7 or sing the song yourself, challenging them to stop at the appropriate times by mixing up the verses.

Child-initiated play

☺ Place the instruments you have introduced indoors or outside where the children can lead the game for themselves or play with an adult.

Extend the activities

🔊 Divide the children into four (or more) groups, each group with different instruments.

Change the instructions using any of the verses from the original song, plus those directed at the groups, eg,

> Shake your shakers in the air,
>
> Tap your beaters on your drum,
>
> Listen to the jingle bells,
>
> Tap the claves together now.

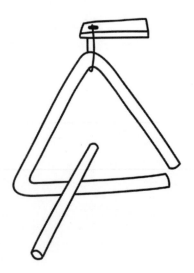

To develop aural memory skills, play a pattern for the children to remember and copy, eg, clap this pattern with your hands:

You: Clap clap clap   Children: clap clap clap

Or play this pattern with your sticks:

You: X   X   X   Children: X   X   X

What you will need

- Sufficient small, hand-held percussion instruments, ideally for each child to have the same, eg, egg shakers.

FOCUS Aspect 2 – General sound discrimination (instrumental sounds):
🎧 Tuning into sounds (auditory discrimination)
🔊 Listening and remembering (auditory memory and sequencing)
☺ Talking about sounds (developing vocabulary and language comprehension)

READY, STEADY, STOP!

Tune: London Bridge

Everybody play with me,
Play with me, play with me,
Everybody play with me,
Ready steady stop!

Everyone play quietly,
Quietly, quietly,
Everyone play quietly,
Ready steady stop!

Everyone play louder now,
Louder now, louder now,
Everyone play louder now,
Ready steady stop!

Everyone play quickly now,
Quickly now, quickly now,
Everyone play quickly now,
Ready steady stop!

Everyone play slowly now,
Slowly now, slowly now,
Everyone play slowly now,
Ready steady stop!

Everyone is growing tired,
Growing tired, growing tired,
Everyone is growing tired,
Ready steady stop!

Everyone is waking up,
Waking up, waking up,
Everyone is waking up,
Now we're wide awake!
(repeat last verse)

SOUND MATCH

Using the song

🎵 Teach the children how to play the sound match game. Play track 8 or sing the song yourself, playing the appropriate instrument from the hidden set in the listening sections of the song.

Choose a child to select the matching instrument and play as prompted in the last line of the song.

Divide the children into two groups: scrapers and drums. This time, when you play the game, the matching group plays their instruments, copying you at the end of the verse.

Child-initiated play

👂 Place matching sets of three different instruments either side of a table with a screen in between so that the children can play the first version of the game in pairs or small groups, with or without singing the song.

Place sets of instrument picture cards with the instruments so that children can order the cards to make sequences, play the game with matching instruments or play the extended version of the game with or without the song.

Extend the activities

🗨 Once the children are familiar with the game, make it more challenging by selecting instruments with more similar sounds, eg, all wooden – claves, castanets, woodblocks; all metal – bells, triangles, cymbals.

Help the children to develop their aural memory skills by playing the game with a sequence of three sounds, eg,

> Listen to the sounds. (shaker drum bell)
>
> What is it you hear? (shaker drum bell)
>
> Listen to the sound waves as they travel to your ear! (shaker drum bell)
>
> Find the matching sounds. (shaker drum bell)
>
> Which instruments could they be? (shaker drum bell)
>
> Listen to the sounds again, then play them after me!
>
> (you play shaker drum bell)
>
> (child plays shaker drum bell)

What you will need

- Sets of instruments sufficient for small groups.
- Prepare two sets of instruments: scraper, drum – one set on view and one set hidden behind a screen.
- Instrument picture cards can be photocopied from Pg 80.

LETTERS AND SOUNDS

FOCUS Aspect 2 – General sound discrimination (instrumental sounds):
🎵 Tuning into sounds (auditory discrimination)
🗨 Listening and remembering (auditory memory and sequencing)
☺ Talking about sounds (developing vocabulary and language comprehension)

SOUND MATCH

Listen to the sound. (scraper)
What is it you hear? (scraper)
Listen to the sound waves
As they travel to your ear! (scraper)
Find the matching sound. (scraper)
Which instrument could it be?
Listen to the sound again, then play it after me!
(you play scraper then child plays scraper)

Listen to the sound. (drum)
What is it you hear? (drum)
Listen to the sound waves
As they travel to your ear! (drum)
Find the matching sound. (drum)
Which instrument could it be?
Listen to the sound again, then play it after me!
(you play drum then child plays drum)

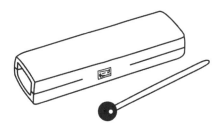

INSTRUMENT PARTY

Using the song

☺ Play the song to the children (track 9), encouraging them to mime playing the instruments mentioned in each verse. Teach them to sing the verses (the instrument sounds), then play the song again and all join in with the verses, miming playing the instruments.

When the children are familiar with the verses, divide them into three instrument groups – shakers, woodblocks and drums. Sing the song all the way through with each group joining in during the verse following the queues in the lyrics. In the instrumental verse at the end of the song, all three groups may join in with the playing!

What you will need

- Shakers, woodblocks or castanets and small hand drums, sufficient for the children to have one instrument each.

Child-initiated play

☺ Place a selection of different instruments or soundmakers indoors or outdoors where the children can play with them freely, eg, pan lids, wooden spoons, plastic beakers, metal bowls.

Encourage children to sing as they play by singing the verses, eg, Rosie's playing on the pan lids, ting ting-a, ting ting-a, ting ting; Ahmed's playing on the chime bars – ding ding-a, ding ding-a, dong dong.

Extend the activities

🔊 When you and the children are familiar with the song, use other instruments you have available to make up new verses, eg, ring, ring, ringing on the jingle bells.

Ask the children to suggest their own made-up sound words for the verses, eg, chunk, chunk, chunk on the tambourine, sss, sss, sss on the maracas.

FOCUS Aspect 2 – General sound discrimination (instrumental sounds):
🔊 Tuning into sounds (auditory discrimination)
🔊 Listening and remembering (auditory memory and sequencing)
☺ Talking about sounds (developing vocabulary and language comprehension)

INSTRUMENT PARTY

Chorus:
Oh, the instruments are having a party,
It's instrument party time.
They play and dance, they dance and play,
Making music all the night and day.
Oh, the instruments are having a party,
It's instrument party time.
So let's join in and sing this song,
And as we sing we'll play along.

Shake, shake, shaking on the shakers,
Shakity, shakity, shake, shake, shake.
Shake, shake, shaking on the shakers,
Shake, shake, shakity shake.

Chorus

Tip, tap, tapping on the woodblocks,
Tappity, tappity, tap, tap, tap.
Tip, tap, tapping on the woodblocks,
Tappity, tappity, tap.

Chorus

Bim, bam, booming on the drumskins,
Boom-di-dee, boom-di-dee, boom, boom, boom.
Bim, bam, booming on the drumskins,
Boom-di-dee, boom-di-dee, boom.
(play all the instruments)

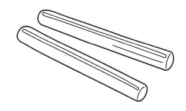

THREE LITTLE PIGS RAP

Using the song

🎧 Play track 10 to listen to the rap version of the three little pigs story, encouraging the children to join in with the vocal sounds in each verse – sh, click, build, climb, splash – and the 'Huff! Puff!' chorus.

Teach them the chorus and encourage them to make their own building actions as they join in with the verses. Over time, the children will learn the rap all the way through.

Child-initiated play

🗨 Collect together props which stimulate children to explore the story, eg, building blocks, straw, sticks, bricks, cardboard boxes, pigs and wolf puppets, plastic cooking pot. Place these outdoors or indoors so that children can re-enact the story.

Extend the activities

☺ Encourage the children to act out the story as they perform the rap.

Discuss the different sounds suggested by the lyrics of the rap. Choose soundmakers or instruments to add sounds to each verse, matching the rhythm pattern of the words, eg,

Straw: egg shakers: *   *   *   *   *

                   sh,   sh,   sh sh sh.

> ### What you will need
>
> • A selection of instruments, eg,
>
> Straw: egg shakers
>
> Sticks: claves
>
> Bricks: flowerpot and beater.

LETTERS AND SOUNDS

FOCUS Aspect 2 – General sound discrimination (instrumental sounds):
🎧 Tuning into sounds (auditory discrimination)
🗨 Listening and remembering (auditory memory and sequencing)
☺ Talking about sounds (developing vocabulary and language comprehension)

24   SINGING PHONICS 1 © HELEN MACGREGOR & CATHERINE BIRT 2008 A & C BLACK PUBLISHERS LTD

THREE LITTLE PIGS RAP

Once upon a time in a faraway wood,
There were three little pigs who decided they could
Build a house, one each:
Straw, sticks, bricks,
But the bad, old wolf was up to his tricks!
So the first little pig built his house of straw.
Sh, sh, sh sh sh.
He put in the windows, he put in the door.
Sh, sh, sh sh sh.

Chorus:
Along came the wolf on his way back from town.
Huff puff, huff puff! I'll blow your house down!
Huff! Puff! I'll blow your house down!
Huff puff, huff puff! I'll blow your house down!
And he did!

So the second little pig built his house of sticks.
Click, click, click click click.
He didn't want straw and he didn't want bricks.
Click, click, click click click.

Chorus

Now the third little pig built his house of bricks.
Build, build, build build build.
He knew that the wolf would be up to his tricks.
Build, build, build build build.
Along came the wolf on his way back from town.
Huff puff, huff puff! I can't blow it down!
Huff! Puff! I can't blow it down!
Huff puff, huff puff! I can't blow it down!
No I couldn't!

The wolf climbed up to the highest spot.
Climb, climb, climb climb climb.
He fell down the chimney and dropped in the pot!
Splash, splash, splash splash splash.
So the three little pigs sent the wolf back to town.
Oink oink oink — you couldn't blow it down!
So the three little pigs sent the wolf back to town.
Oink oink oink — you couldn't blow it down!
No, you couldn't!

SUPER SINGERS!

Using the song

♪ Play track 11 or sing the song yourself, showing the children the actions and encouraging them to join in with the movements. Teach them the words and actions of the chorus, then each verse, noticing that it is only the first line of each verse that changes.

When you and the children are ready, perform the whole song with actions, indoors or outdoors.

Child-initiated play

🗪 Encourage the children to explore other actions independently or in small groups to make a new body percussion dance or song.

Extend the activities

☺ Try performing the actions of the first three lines of a verse or the chorus while using 'thinking voices' (singing the song silently in your head). Can the children perform the body actions in the correct sequence?

LETTERS AND SOUNDS

FOCUS Aspect 3 – General sound discrimination (body percussion):
♪ Tuning into sounds (auditory discrimination)
🗪 Listening and remembering (auditory memory and sequencing)
☺ Talking about sounds (developing vocabulary and language comprehension)

SUPER SINGERS!
Tune: Pop goes the weasel

Chorus:
Head and nose and shoulders and toes,
Legs and arms and fingers,
Bend and stretch and wriggle and shake,
We're super singers!

Stamp your feet down onto the floor,
Clap your hands together,
Hold your breath — and blow it out — ooooooh!
Light as a feather.

Chorus

Bend your knees then turn around,
Clap your hands together,
Hold your breath — and blow it out — ooooooh!
Light as a feather.

Chorus

Hands on waist and wiggle your hips,
Clap your hands together,
Hold your breath — and blow it out — ooooooh!
Light as a feather.

CHICKEN LICKEN NUMBERS

Using the song

🎧 Listen to track 12, performing the actions suggested by the lyrics for the children to copy. Play it again, encouraging the children to join in with the counting and action words at first, then gradually with the whole chant.

Child-initiated play

🎧 Place a set of number cards (one to ten) and ten toy hens (or picture cards) along with egg shakers for the children to explore playing numbers patterns and/or saying the chant. You can photocopy the illustration of Chicken Licken (opposite page).

Extend the activities

🗣 When the children know the chant well, perform it without the CD, indoors or outdoors. Add claps on each number.

Divide into two groups. Give Group one egg shakers to play, and all say the chant as the players practise adding one shake on each number.

What you will need

- A set of number cards (one to ten) and ten toy hens (or picture cards – see opposite page).

- Egg shakers

- Photocopies of Singing Phonics 1 illustrations can be used – see list of illustrations at the back of the book.

One,   two,   three,   four,   five.

Group two performs the chant with actions as the players add the instrument sounds to each counting section.

FOCUS Aspect 3 – General sound discrimination (body percussion):
🎧 Tuning into sounds (auditory discrimination)
🗣 Listening and remembering (auditory memory and sequencing)
☺ Talking about sounds (developing vocabulary and language comprehension)

CHICKEN LICKEN NUMBERS

Chicken Licken numbers count to ten,
Chicken Licken numbers then do it again.
Stamp on the floor and jiggle and jive,
One, two, three, four, five.
Stamp, stamp, stamp, stamp, stamp
Jump in the chicken car and drive, drive, drive,
One, two, three, four, five.
Drive, drive, drive, drive, drive.
Flap your wings like a mother hen,
Six, seven, eight, nine, ten!
Flap, flap, flap, flap, flap.
Do the Chicken licken dance and do it again.
Six, seven, eight, nine, ten.
Bck, bck, bck! bck! bck!

NOISY NEIGHBOURS

13

Using the song

🎵 Act out the song as you listen to track 13, encouraging the children to join in. Teach the children the song: at first, adults can take the role of the noisy neighbours (the male singer) and the children sing their parts (the female voice).

When the game is familiar, the children can be divided into two groups and allocated the role of children or noisy neighbours. They then perform the song and actions, taking it in turns to sing the two alternate parts. Swap over so that everyone has a chance to be a noisy neighbour!

Child-initiated play

🗨 Set up a doll's house with play people and props, or a home corner with rooms and furniture so that the children can sing and re-enact the verses they have made up – and make up more!

Extend the activities

🎵 Ask the children to suggest other verses and sounds, eg,

Brushing teeth: brush

Munching cornflakes: chomp

Waking up: yawn

Washing hands: splash

What you will need

• A doll's house with play people and props, or a home corner with rooms and furniture.

LETTERS AND SOUNDS

FOCUS Aspect 3 – General sound discrimination (body percussion):
🎵 Tuning into sounds (auditory discrimination)
🗨 Listening and remembering (auditory memory and sequencing)
☺ Talking about sounds (developing vocabulary and language comprehension)

30   SINGING PHONICS 1 © HELEN MACGREGOR & CATHERINE BIRT 2008 A & C BLACK PUBLISHERS LTD

NOISY NEIGHBOURS

Tune: Skip to my lou

Children:
Noisy neighbours, please be quiet,
Noisy neighbours, please be quiet,
Noisy neighbours, please be quiet,
We are trying to sleep! Ssssh!
Shh, shh, please be quiet,
Shh, shh, please be quiet,
Shh, shh, please be quiet,
We are trying to sleep! Ssssh!

Noisy neighbours:
Noisy neighbours, stamping feet, (x3)
Waking up the children.
Stamp, stamp, stamping feet, (x3)
Waking up the children.

Children:
Noisy neighbours, please be quiet, (x3)
We are trying to sleep! Ssssh!

Noisy neighbours:
Noisy neighbours, clapping hands, (x3)
Waking up the children.
Clap clap clapping hands, (x3)
Waking up the children.

Children:
Noisy neighbours, go to bed! (x3)
Peace and quiet at last — aaah!

SINGING PHONICS 1 © HELEN MACGREGOR & CATHERINE BIRT 2008 A & C BLACK PUBLISHERS LTD

COPYCATS

Using the song

🎵 Sing the song yourself or use track 14. Perform each of the actions suggested in the game, encouraging the children to copy, following the instructions.

Child-initiated play

🎵 Place pairs of picture cards showing the patterns you have performed in the song where children can play them in pairs, taking it in turns to be the leader and the copycat.

Extend the activities

🗣 Develop the song by performing different sounds for the children to copy, eg, quiet or loud sounds, new rhythms on instruments.

Develop the children's listening skills and aural memory by hiding when you perform the sound. This time they listen and copy without seeing what you are doing. Change the words to:

> Copycats, copycats,
>
> Can you copy copy me, copycats?
>
> Listen very closely then you do the same!

What you will need

- Picture cards for actions (you can photocopy illustrations and create picture cards – see illustration list on inside back cover).

FOCUS Aspect 3 – General sound discrimination (body percussion):
🎵 Tuning into sounds (auditory discrimination)
🗣 Listening and remembering (auditory memory and sequencing)
☺ Talking about sounds (developing vocabulary and language comprehension)

COPYCATS

Copycats, copycats,
Can you copy, copy me, copycats?
Watch very closely, then you do the same!

You: Clap clap clap   Children: Clap clap clap
Let's clap hands, copycats.
You: Clap clap clap   Children: Clap clap clap
Yeah, yeah, we did the same!

Copycats, copycats,
Can you copy, copy me, copycats?
Watch very closely, then you do the same!

You: (tap feet) X X X   Children X X X
Tap our feet, copy cats.
You: X X X   Children X X X
Yeah, yeah, we did the same!

Copycats, copycats,
Can you copy, copy me, copycats?
Watch very closely, then you do the same!

You: (click tongue) X X X   Children X X X
Click our tongues, copy cats.
You: X X X   Children X X X
Yeah, yeah, we did the same!

HICKORY DICKORY DONG

Using the song

🐦 Say together the original rhyme, Hickory dickory dock, and discuss its meaning. Ask the children to listen to the song by singing it yourself or playing track 15, encouraging them to join in with the repeated phrases as they become familiar. Gradually learn the verses one at a time, then sing the whole song together, adding any actions suggested by the words of each verse.

What you will need

• Puppets, props, toys or dressing up items to symbolise a variety of favourite nursery rhymes.

• High-quality poetry, verse, nursery rhyme books and tapes.

• Picture cards and rhyming word cards.

Child-initiated play

☺ Ensure children have access to high quality poetry, verse, nursery rhyme books and tapes as well as puppets, props and dressing up items to help them to recall their favourite rhymes.

Place picture cards and rhyming word cards where the children can play with them, eg,

> Bee: tree, sea, flea, knee, three
>
> Clock: sock, rock, knock, lock
>
> Hen: pen, men, ten
>
> Dog: log, frog

Can they sort the picture cards into rhyming sets?

Extend the activities

👂 When the song is well known, make up more verses with more than one set of rhyming words per verse to give the children experience of more rhyming words, eg,

> Hickory dickory den,
> My hen sat on ten men,
> Well fancy that! A pet hen hat!
> Hickory dickory den.
>
> Hickory dickory dog,
> The frog jumped on the log,
> A fish swam by and winked his eye,
> Hickory dickory dog.

FOCUS Aspect 4 – Rhythm and rhyme:
 👂 Tuning into sounds (auditory discrimination)
 🐦 Listening and remembering (auditory memory and sequencing)
 ☺ Talking about sounds (developing vocabulary and language comprehension)

HICKORY DICKORY DONG
Tune: Hickory dickory dock

Hickory dickory dong,
Let's sing a silly song,
A silly song that won't take long,
Hickory dickory dong.

Hickory dickory dee,
Here comes a bumble bee,
Oh bumble bee, please don't sting me!
Hickory dickory dee.

Hickory dickory dong,
Another silly song,
A silly song that won't take long,
Hickory dickory dong.

Hickory dickory dum,
A bee just loves to hum,
It loves to hum, so does my Mum!
Hickory dickory dum.

Hickory dickory dong,
Another silly song,
A silly song that won't take long,
Hickory dickory dong.

Hickory dickory dock,
My Mum hums pop and rock,
Pop and rock, around the clock,
Hickory dickory dock!

NEW PLACES

(16)

Using the song

🎧 Listen to the song on track 16. Talk about one verse and chorus at a time, discussing possible actions. Encourage the children to move as they act out the words in each verse, and join in singing the chorus as it becomes familiar over a period of time.

Talk about the different types of journeys and transport described in each verse of the song.

Child-initiated play

☺ Leave toys and props for the children to explore freely through role-play and movement. Encourage the children to use similar chorus patterns when playing with indoor or outdoor toys, such as 'red bus, red bus....' or 'big trike, big trike....'

Extend the activities

🗩 Act out the verses with groups of children indoors or outdoors, using whole body movements.

Sailboat: use a cardboard box and pretend to sail in a boat, or sing as you play in the water play area using a toy boat, dolphins and octopus.

Tube train: move through a play tunnel.

Big wheel: make large circular movements from high to low.

Spaceship: play with space toys in the sand tray, making a lunar landscape or make a spaceship with armholes from a large cardboard box so a child can wear it for a trip into space!

Make up new choruses with the children, eg, 'lorry, lorry.....' or 'digger, digger....'

What you will need

• Toys and props (see Child-initiated play section).

FOCUS Aspect 4 – Rhythm and rhyme:
🎧 Tuning into sounds (auditory discrimination)
🗩 Listening and remembering (auditory memory and sequencing)
☺ Talking about sounds (developing vocabulary and language comprehension)

NEW PLACES
Tune: My bonnie lies over the ocean

Oh, have you been out in a sailboat,
To float on the ocean so blue?
Where octopus live underwater,
And dolphins swim following you?
Sailboat, sailboat,
Oh come on a sailboat with me, with me.
Sailboat, sailboat,
So many new places to see!

Oh, have you been down in a tube train,
To travel fast, deep underground?
Just look on the map for the station,
The Circle line goes round and round.
Tube train, tube train,
Oh come on a tube train with me, with me.
Tube train, tube train,
So many new places to see!

Oh, have you been round on a big wheel,
Up high as it turns in the air?
Look down on the fairground below you,
And feel the wind blow through your hair.
Big wheel, big wheel,
Oh come on a big wheel with me, with me.
Big wheel, big wheel,
So many new places to see!

Oh, have you been up in a spaceship,
Far out into space to see Mars?
Countdown when it's time for a landing,
To visit the moon and the stars.
Spaceship, spaceship,
Oh come on a spaceship with me, with me.
Spaceship, spaceship,
So many new places to see!

EASY PEASY

Using the song

🗣 Hide a mixture of objects or picture cards for CVC words (see What you will need box for ideas) in a hat. Choose a child to wave a toy wand over the hat as you sing the magic spell or play track 17 and encourage them to name the object as they pull it out for everyone to see. Everyone repeats the name of the object. Repeat the song with each new object, checking for rhyming words, for instance cat-bat-rat / dog-log-frog / can-pan-man.

Child-initiated play

☺ Leave the hat around with several rhyming objects and/or pictures for children to use independently.

Hide large laminated pictures of well-known rhymes and verses around the indoor and outdoor environments. Children will find and use these in their play once familiar with them.

Extend the activities

☺ Work with the children to make up their own rhymes. Nursery rhymes can be used as a basis for these as the name of the character, action or object can be changed, eg,

'Humpty Dumpty' could become 'Henry Penry' or 'Dizzy Dozy',

'sat on a wall and had a great fall' could become 'jumped on a stool and played the fool'.

Encourage children to tap out the rhythms of the words of the song, on commercial or home-made instruments:

Claves: *   *   *   *   *   *   *   *   *   *   *

    Ea- sy pea-sy le-mon squee-zy, Flee fly   flo.

Tap out rhythms of the first lines of well-known nursery rhymes and ask the children to guess which ones you are doing.

FOCUS Aspect 4 – Rhythm and rhyme:

🎵 Tuning into sounds (auditory discrimination)

🐛 Listening and remembering (auditory memory and sequencing)

☺ Talking about sounds (developing vocabulary and language comprehension)

What you will need

- A hat containing a selection of toys or picture cards for CVC (consonant, vowel, consonant) words, eg, cat, rat, hat, mat; pig, wig; dog, log, frog; man, pan, fan; box, fox, socks, clocks.

- Large laminated pictures of well-known rhymes and verses.

EASY PEASY

Easy peasy lemon squeezy,
Flee fly flo.
Time for a rhyming trick,
Here we go!
Wibble wobble dibble dobble,
This and that.
Can you find the things that rhyme
Inside the hat?

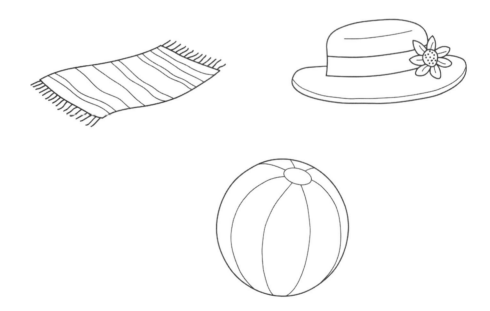

DAVE THE BAT

18

Using the song

🔊 Listen to the song on track 18, joining in with the repeating pattern in the last two lines of each verse.

Talk about which words rhyme:

cave and Dave

long and song

night and sight

Ask the children to think of actions to go with words in the chorus and sing the song again until it becomes more familiar.

Child-initiated play

☺ The role-play area could become a cave with bats made by the children using the area. Pictures and toys representing other cave dwellers such as bears, badgers and spiders as well as story books, poetry and non-fiction books containing photographs of cave dwellers could also be left in the role-play area. Children could act out stories and scenarios in their cave, making the appropriate noises as they play.

Extend the activities

🔊 Read and tell well-known rhymes and stories related to creatures living in caves. There are many examples of bear stories and rhymes, eg, 'We're going on a bear hunt' by Michael Rose, 'Teddy bear, teddy bear' and 'Can't you sleep, little bear?' by Martin Waddell.

Extend this to well-known rhymes and stories about other animals. Children can re-enact stories and rhymes and begin to make up their own rhymes with help from adults.

What you will need

• Pictures and toys representing cave-dwelling creatures (see Child-initiated play).

• Stories and rhymes about cave-dwelling animals, eg, bears, bats.

FOCUS Aspect 4 – Rhythm and rhyme:
🔊 Tuning into sounds (auditory discrimination)
🔊 Listening and remembering (auditory memory and sequencing)
☺ Talking about sounds (developing vocabulary and language comprehension)

DAVE THE BAT

I have a little bat and he lives in a cave,
He's my furry friend and his name is Dave.
He hangs from the rafters all day long,
And as he hangs he sings this song:

Flip flap, blink blink, squeak squeak!
Flip flap, blink blink, squeak squeak!

Dave sleeps all day and he wakes at night,
He uses radar instead of sight.
Eating insects all night long,
And as he flies he sings this song:

Flip flap, blink blink, squeak squeak!
Flip flap, blink blink, squeak squeak!

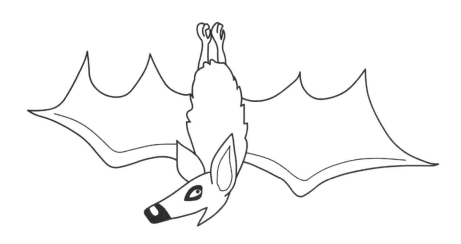

HUBBLE BUBBLE POT

Using the song

🔊 Listen to track 19. Place picture cards or objects starting with the same sound to match each verse in a pan or cooking pot.

Repeat the chant along with the children, using the same beginning sounds until it becomes familiar to them. Gradually introduce new beginning sounds, encouraging them to look for appropriate objects/pictures from around the indoor and outdoor environments.

Play the game again using objects or pictures starting with the same sound to put in the pot and singing the appropriate words yourself.

Child-initiated play

☺ Leave the pot and a variety of objects, pictures, name cards beginning with same sound around for children to play with independently. Pictures, objects, names could be changed regularly and an 'odd one out' could be introduced.

Extend the activities

🔊 Put children's names which start with the same sound into the pot, eg, Jimmy, John, Jasmine or Cherie, Charlotte. Practitioners could adapt the game to use for children's self-registration.

What you will need

- Picture cards or objects starting with the same sound for each verse. Photocopy and use some illustrations from the book (see illustration list at the back of the book). Letter cards, Pgs 79–80.
- Pan or cooking pot.

FOCUS Aspect 5 – Alliteration:
🔊 Tuning into sounds (auditory discrimination)
🔊 Listening and remembering (auditory memory and sequencing)
☺ Talking about sounds (developing vocabulary and language comprehension)

HUBBLE BUBBLE POT

Hubble bubble hubble bubble,
What's in the pot?
Hubble bubble hubble bubble,
What have we got?
Bug, ball, beetle, brush,
That's what we've got in the pot!

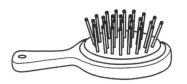

Hubble bubble hubble bubble,
What's in the pot?
Hubble bubble hubble bubble,
What have we got?
Cat, cream, candle, cup,
That's what we've got in the pot!

Hubble bubble hubble bubble,
What's in the pot?
Hubble bubble hubble bubble,
What have we got?
Flies, flower, fork, feet,
That's what we've got in the pot!

Hubble bubble hubble bubble,
What's in the pot?
Hubble bubble hubble bubble,
What have we got?
Peach, potato, pineapple, pear,
That's what we've got in the pot!

SOCKS AND SNAKES

(20)

Using the song

🎵 Listen to the song on track 20. Talk about how many of the words in the first verse begin with the same sound sss. Join in with the song, making the letter sounds at the end of each verse.

Make up new verses with the children, eg,

Goats and grubs and Goldilocks

Hair and house and holiday

Jam and juice and Jamaquacks

Kite and kick and kangaroo

Lick and loop and lemonade

Moon and mouse and marmalade

Nut and nail and nightingale

Pizza, plum and pineapple

Child-initiated play

☺ Encourage children to play singing/action games indoors and outdoors, particularly those using alliteration, for instance 'a sailor went to sea, sea, sea, to see what he could see see see, and all that he could see, see, see, was the bottom of the deep blue sea, sea, sea'.

Extend the activities

☺ Use the children's names to create silly alliterative phrases:

David's dog drinks daffodils

Helen's horse hears hurricanes

Ben's bat bottles blackberries

Catherine's clock cries currant cakes

Martin's mouse makes molehill maps

Nicky's nurse needs nitrogen.

FOCUS Aspect 5 – Alliteration:

🎵 Tuning into sounds (auditory discrimination)

🐛 Listening and remembering (auditory memory and sequencing)

☺ Talking about sounds (developing vocabulary and language comprehension)

SOCKS AND SNAKES
Tune: London Bridge

Socks and snakes and sausages,
Sausages, sausages,
Socks and snakes and sausages,
s s ss.

Bats and bears and bandicoots,
Bandicoots, bandicoots,
Bats and bears and bandicoots,
b b bb.

Cats and cakes and crocodiles,
Crocodiles, crocodiles,
Cats and cakes and crocodiles,
c c cc.

Ducks and Dads and dinosaurs,
Dinosaurs, dinosaurs,
Ducks and Dads and dinosaurs,
d d dd.

Fish and feet and friendly frogs,
Friendly frogs, friendly frogs,
Fish and feet and friendly frogs,
f f ff.

Socks and snakes and sausages,
Sausages, sausages,
Socks and snakes and sausages,
s s ss!

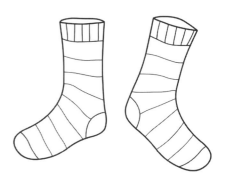

PINKY PARTY PIG

Using the song

🔊 Place picture cards of the animals (pig, snake and goat) or toys where the children can see them. Point to the matching card/object in each verse. Can the children remember the names of the three animals?

Sing the song again, encouraging the children to join in with the animals' names and the letter sounds.

Child-initiated play

☺ Place the rhyming objects or picture cards where the children can explore the game or sing the song by themselves or in small groups.

Extend the activities

☺ When the children are familiar with the song, make up new alliterative verses, eg,

> Funny fish and frog
>
> Blue balloon and ball
>
> Sleepy, slimy slug
>
> Happy holiday

Make the song more challenging for those children who are ready to explore alliteration in phase 2:

> Sing the sound that ends these words:
> Cat and pot and net.
> Sing the sound that ends these words:
> Cat and pot and net.
> With a t t here and a t t there,
> Here a t, there a t, everywhere a t t.
> Sing the sound that ends these words:
> Cat and pot and net.

What you will need

• Picture cards/toys representing the animals in the song and others to make up new verses.

FOCUS Aspect 5 – Alliteration:
🔊 Tuning into sounds (auditory discrimination)
🔊 Listening and remembering (auditory memory and sequencing)
☺ Talking about sounds (developing vocabulary and language comprehension)

PINKY PARTY PIG
Tune: Old MacDonald

Sing the sound that starts these words:
Pinky party pig.
Sing the sound that starts these words:
Pinky party pig.
With a p p here and a p p there,
Here a p, there a p, everywhere a p p.
Sing the sound that starts these words:
Pinky party pig.

Sing the sound that starts these words:
Silly Sidney snake.
Sing the sound that starts these words:
Silly Sidney snake.
With a ss here and a ss there,
Here a ss, there a ss, everywhere a ss ss.
Sing the sound that starts these words:
Silly Sidney snake.

Sing the sound that starts these words:
Giddy Gertie goat.
Sing the sound that starts these words:
Giddy Gertie goat.
With a g g here and a g g there,
Here a g, there a g everywhere a g g.
Sing the sound that starts these words:
Giddy Gertie goat.

SINGING PHONICS 1 © HELEN MACGREGOR & CATHERINE BIRT 2008 A & C BLACK PUBLISHERS LTD

SOUND BOX

Using the song

👂 Show the children four picture cards/objects that begin with the same sound, for instance dog, door, dish and drink (as in the chorus and verse 1). Talk about the sound they all begin with and then listen to the chorus and first verse (track 22). Sing the chorus and first verse with the children.

Gradually build up the song in this way, talking about the beginning sounds and enunciating these correctly in each chorus and verse.

Child-initiated play

☺ Leave the box and hide a small selection of pictures/objects, beginning with the same sound, in the outdoor or indoor area for the children to discover and play with independently. Encourage the children to search for more objects/ pictures to include in the game.

Extend the activities

☺ Encourage children to help you to have fun making up your own pattern of four words beginning with same sound, for instance a fish and a fox and a fan and a feather...no rhyming is necessary for this activity.

What you will need

- A decorated box containing picture cards of the alliterative nouns mentioned in each verse.

- Extra picture cards or objects beginning with the same sound to extend the game, eg, fish, fox, fan, feather.

FOCUS Aspect 5 – Alliteration:
 👂 Tuning into sounds (auditory discrimination)
 👂 Listening and remembering (auditory memory and sequencing)
 ☺ Talking about sounds (developing vocabulary and language comprehension)

SOUND BOX

Tune: Here we go round the mulberry bush

What do we have in our sound box today,
Sound box today, sound box today?
What do we have in our sound box today?
Things that begin with d.

A dog and a door, a dish and a drink,
Dog and a door, a dish and a drink,
Dog and a door, a dish and a drink,
Things that begin with d.

What do we have in our sound box today,
Sound box today, sound box today?
What do we have in our sound box today?
Things that begin with n.

A nut and a nail, a needle and net,
Nut and a nail, a needle and net,
Nut and a nail, a needle and net,
Things that begin with n.

What do we have in our sound box today,
Sound box today, sound box today?
What do we have in our sound box today?
Things that begin with t.

A toy and a train, a tractor, a tin,
Toy and a train, a tractor, a tin,
Toy and a train, a tractor, a tin,
Things that begin with t.

MY LITTLE EAR

Using the song

🎵 Listen to the song (track 23). Have objects or picture cards in a bag or cloth box to pull out as they are mentioned in the song. Discuss the sound that the objects in each verse begin with.

Play or sing the song again so children become familiar with the idea of listening to the beginning sounds and understanding that these are all the same.

Child-initiated play

☺ Leave a tray or hoop and a cover with some objects beginning with the same sound for children to use indoors or outdoors.

Extend the activities

🗨 Play the game using your own collection of objects or pictures, making up new verses to match.

Play 'Odd one out' with objects or pictures – repeat the game but introduce an odd one out and ask the children to discuss which one is odd and why.

Play 'Kim's Game': place objects beginning with the same sound on a tray or inside a hoop. The children look at each object, saying its name. Cover the tray/hoop and remove one object. The children guess which one is missing.

FOCUS Aspect 5 – Alliteration:
🎵 Tuning into sounds (auditory discrimination)
🗨 Listening and remembering (auditory memory and sequencing)
☺ Talking about sounds (developing vocabulary and language comprehension)

MY LITTLE EAR

I can hear with my little ear,
Something that starts with 'b'.
It isn't a bag, it isn't a box,
So what do you think it could be?
It's a.... bear!

I can hear with my little ear,
Something that starts with 'c'.
It isn't a comb, it isn't a cup,
So what do you think it could be?
It's a ..... carrot!

I can hear with my little ear,
Something that starts with 'g'.
It isn't a girl, it isn't a glass,
So what do you think it could be?
It's a.... glove!

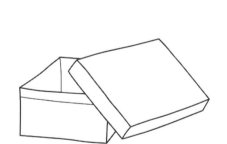

OUT TO PLAY

24

Using the song

𝄞 Listen to the song on track 24, demonstrating the actions suggested by the words and encouraging the children to join in with them.

Sing it again yourself, or, using the CD this time, ask the children to join in with the repeating words, sounds and actions in each verse as they gradually become more familiar with the song.

Finally, perform the whole song with actions.

Child-initiated play

☺ Encourage the children to sing the song for themselves as they play outside by singing appropriate words when you observe them at play, eg, riding on a bike, ding, ding, ding, ding.

Extend the activities

🐦 Explore more word patterns and sounds by making up new verses to sing with the children as they are involved in indoor or outdoor activities, eg,

Driving in a car: vroom, vroom, vroom, vroom.

Moving like a train: chuff, chuff, chuff, chuff.

Climbing up the steps: 1 step, 2 steps, 3 steps, 4 steps.

Stirring with a spoon: mix-a, mix-a, mix-a, mix-a.

Discuss other ways of singing the song with the children to explore different themes, eg,

Animals: Buzzing like a bee / Barking like a dog

Moods: Feeling really sad / Sounding really cross

Home: Ticking like a clock / Humming like a fridge

FOCUS Aspect 6 – Voice sounds:
  𝄞 Tuning into sounds (auditory discrimination)
  🐦 Listening and remembering (auditory memory and sequencing)
  ☺ Talking about sounds (developing vocabulary and language comprehension)

OUT TO PLAY

Tune: Jelly on a plate

Going out to play,
Going out to play.
Hooray, hooray, hooray, hooray!
Going out to play.

Bouncing like a ball,
Bouncing like a ball.
Boing, boing, boing, boing,
Bouncing like a ball.

Sitting on a swing,
Sitting on a swing.
Whoooosh, whooosh,
Sitting on a swing.

Going down the slide,
Going down the slide.
Wheeeeeeeeeeeeeee!
Going down the slide.

Digging in the soil,
Digging in the soil.
Clunk, clunk, clunk, clunk,
Digging in the soil.

Hiding in the den,
Hiding in the den.
Shh, shh, shh, shh,
Hiding in the den.

Going out to play,
Going out to play.
Hooray, hooray, hooray, hooray!
Going out to play.

SAY IT!

25

Using the song

👂 Listen to the song (track 25). Discuss how we can make our voices do different things.

Chant the verse for the children without the CD, using your own voice expressively to describe the different qualities mentioned in the lyrics. Notice the differences when we speak in low voices or high voices, when we speak slowly or quickly and the different qualities of posh, sad, quietly, glad.

Chant the verse again, encouraging children to think about how facial expressions often mirror what we do when we use our voices in different ways.

Child-initiated play

☺ Have rhyme or song sacks available for the children to play with. These could contain a variety of items such as illustrated rhymes on card, appropriate puppets, toys, props or dressing up items for re-enacting the rhyme and a recording of the rhyme.

Extend the activities

🗫 Use other songs or rhymes to practise using different voices, for instance nursery rhymes such as Humpty Dumpty said with sad voices or happy voices. Discuss which sound best and why. Encourage children to think of other ways in which they could use their voices and mouth movements to make interesting sounds, such as blowing, sucking, making animal noises (buzz, meow), or even ticking loudly like a big clock or softly like a tiny clock.

What you will need

• Sacks containing a variety of items, eg, illustrated rhymes on card, appropriate puppets, toys, props or dressing up items for re-enacting the rhyme and a recording of the rhyme (for Child-initiated play).

FOCUS Aspect 6 – Voice sounds:
👂 Tuning into sounds (auditory discrimination)
🗫 Listening and remembering (auditory memory and sequencing)
☺ Talking about sounds (developing vocabulary and language comprehension)

SAY IT!

Say it in a high voice.
Then say it very low.
Say it very quickly.
Then say it very slow.
Say it in a posh voice.
Say it sounding sad.
Say it very quietly.
Then say it sounding glad.
(repeat)

PROFESSOR BRAIN'S AMAZING MACHINE 26

Using the song

🎵 Play the song to the children, encouraging them to add actions and echo-sing the machine patterns in the copy sections. What do they notice about the patterns as the song progresses? (The new patterns are added in front of the old patterns one by one to make a sequence.)

Help the children to remember the sequence by practising each one with actions – you sing it first, then the children copy. Gradually build up the whole sequence and sing the whole song.

Encourage the children in the role-play of Professor Brain as they mime building and operating the machine in the chorus.

When the song is familiar, you may like to divide the children into two groups and ask one group to lead for the other to echo-sing the machine patterns.

What you will need

• Bricks, junk or other construction materials (for Child-initiated play)

Child-initiated play

💬 Provide bricks, junk or other construction materials for the children to design and build Professor Brain's amazing machine. Encourage them to make their own sound patterns for the machine they have built and share these with other children.

Extend the activities

💬 Talk about the different patterns of sound and ask them what they think the machine is doing for each. Ask the children to try out their own actions for each of the patterns as they sing the song, eg,

Whirr, whirr, click, click: fingers of both hands circle then press button.

Share some of their ideas and try them out together as you sing the song all the way through.

FOCUS Aspect 6 – Voice sounds:
🎵 Tuning into sounds (auditory discrimination)
💬 Listening and remembering (auditory memory and sequencing)
☺ Talking about sounds (developing vocabulary and language comprehension)

PROFESSOR BRAIN'S AMAZING MACHINE

Chorus:
Professor Brain built a great machine
Made out of metal and tin.
It can do anything that you ask it to,
Just press the buttons in,
And it goes...

Whirr, whirr, click, click, whirr, whirr, click, click.
It's the most amazing machine!

Chorus:
Professor Brain...

Beep, beep, sh, sh, sh, beep, beep, sh, sh, sh.
Whirr, whirr, click, click, whirr, whirr, click, click.
It's the most amazing machine!

Chorus:
Professor Brain...

Boom diddy boom diddy boom boom boom,
Boom diddy boom diddy boom boom, boom.
Beep, beep, sh, sh, sh, beep, beep, sh, sh, sh.
Whirr, whirr, click, click, whirr, whirr, click, click.
It's the most amazing machine!

Chorus:
Professor Brain...

Chugga wugga, (x4)
Chugga wugga, (x4)
Boom diddy boom diddy boom boom boom,
Boom diddy boom diddy boom boom, boom.
Beep, beep, sh, sh, sh, beep, beep, sh, sh, sh.
Whirr, whirr, click, click, whirr, whirr, click, click.
It's the most amazing machine!

SINGALONGA NOAH

27

Using the song

🎵 Play track 27 and all listen to the song. Tell the story of Noah's Ark, or ask the children to re-tell it if it is already familiar.

Play the song again, demonstrating the actions, encouraging the children to join in with actions and animal sounds.

Sing the song to the children a verse at a time, exploring whole body actions for each animal and practising the sound patterns as they build up into a sequence of four animals in the last verse.

Child-initiated play

Provide opportunities for 'small world' play. Make a zoo, farm or Noah's Ark play area with toy animals matching those mentioned in the song so that the children can experiment with their own animal sounds.

Encourage the children to sing and play action songs and rhymes during child-initiated time by providing appropriate books, rhymes, story sacks, taped songs, dressing up items, role-play areas indoors and outdoors.

Extend the activities

🎵 Help the children to make a large wall frieze or collage showing all the animals mentioned in the song. When it is complete, ask the children to make the matching animal sounds as you point to each animal in turn. Choose a child to be the conductor and point animals in any order.

Divide the children into four groups: cocks and hens, lions and tigers, monkeys and birds.

This time, when the conductor points to the animals on the frieze, only the matching group makes its sound. What happens if you have two conductors? (You will hear two animal sounds at the same time.)

What you will need

• Materials to create a 'small world' play area (for Child-initiated play).

• Materials to build a large frieze or collage showing all the animals mentioned in the song to extend the activity.

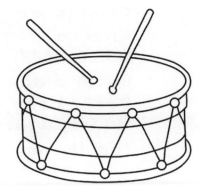

FOCUS Aspect 6 – Voice sounds:
🎵 Tuning into sounds (auditory discrimination)
Listening and remembering (auditory memory and sequencing)
☺ Talking about sounds (developing vocabulary and language comprehension)

SINGALONGA NOAH

Here come the animals two by two.
Cockerels crowing: 'a cock a doodle doo'.
The hens flap their wings and scratch their feet.
Singalonga Noah and bop to the beat.
Cock a doodle, cock a doodle, cock a doodle-doo,
Cock a doodle, cock a doodle, cock a doodle-doo.
Flap your wings and scratch your feet,
Singalonga Noah and bop to the beat.

Here come the animals four by four.
Lions and tigers, roar roar roar.
On the prowl for a treat to eat.
Singalonga Noah and bop to the beat.
Cock a doodle, cock a doodle, roar, roar, roar.
Cock a doodle, cock a doodle, roar, roar, roar.
On the prowl for a treat to eat,
Singalonga Noah and bop to the beat.

Here come the animals six by six.
Scritch scratch monkeys with their trickety tricks.
Baby monkeys jumping, they're so sweet.
Singalonga Noah and bop to the beat.
Cock a doodle, roar, roar, scritch, scratch, scritch,
Cock a doodle, roar, roar, scritch, scratch, scritch.
Baby monkeys jumping, they're so sweet.
Singalonga Noah and bop to the beat.

Here come the animals eight by eight.
Tweet tweet birdies, sitting on the gate.
Dance with the birdies, tweet, tweet, tweet.
Singalonga Noah and bop to the beat.
Cock a doodle, roar, roar, scritch scratch, tweet,
Cock a doodle, roar, roar, scritch scratch, tweet.
Dance with the birdies tweet, tweet, tweet,
Singalonga Noah and bop to the beat.

MAKE THE SOUNDS

Using the song

🎵 Listen to the song on track 28 and sing along with it, modelling clearly how to say each segmented phoneme as it is repeated.

Show the children a picture card or the three letter cards for 'man' and practise saying each of the letter sounds together. Repeat with the words in the other verses. Play the track again and ask the children to join in making the sounds in lines two and four of each verse as you point to the letter cards one by one.

Child-initiated play

☺ Leave the letter cards where the children can order them to form the CVC (consonant, vowel, consonant) words from the song and practise saying the phonemes by themselves.

Later on you may like to introduce more familiar CVC words, using picture or letter cards to prompt the children in singing their own verses, eg, Can you say the sounds in cat?

Extend the activity

☺ Place a selection of new objects or picture cards of your own choice in a bag. Play a game to extend the children's experience of segmenting simple words as you make up more verses of the song. Take out a new object or card from the bag and sing the question, eg,

Oh can you make the sounds in hen? To prompt the children to orally segment the phonemes:

h-e-n, h-e-n.....

<blockquote>
What you will need

- Letter or picture cards for each for the four words: m a n, b e d, p i g, t o p.

- A selection of new objects or picture cards for CVC words of your own choice.
</blockquote>

FOCUS Aspect 7 – Oral blending and segmenting

🎵 Tuning into sounds (auditory discrimination)

🐾 Listening and remembering (auditory memory and sequencing)

☺ Talking about sounds (developing vocabulary and language comprehension)

MAKE THE SOUNDS
Tune: The wheels on the bus

Oh, can you make the sounds in man?
M-a-n, m-a-n.
Can you make the sounds in man?
M-a-n.

Oh, can you make the sounds in bed?
B-e-d, b-e-d.
Can you make the sounds in bed?
B-e-d.

Oh, can you make the sounds in pig?
P-i-g, p-i-g.
Can you make the sounds in pig?
P-i-g.

Oh, can you make the sounds in top?
T-o-p, t-o-p.
Can you make the sounds in top?
T-o-p.

TALKING BAG

Using the song

☺ Listen to the song on track 29.

Ensure the children understand the meaning of sound talk (segmenting the separate sounds or phonemes in a word). Give children practice at segmenting c-a-t and blending back together as cat.

Sing along with the song, pulling the cat picture card, toy or object out of bag as you sing.

Ask a volunteer to segment and blend the word and ask the rest of the children to copy them.

Repeat the game using other objects from the bag.

What you will need

• An attractive bag containing objects, toys or picture cards, eg, cat, dog, pig, fish, shell, tap, pan, dish, zip, top, pot, sock, bus, peg, man, duck, get, mat.

• More complex objects/picture cards/word cards to extend the activity.

Child-initiated play

☺ Leave the bag and objects/picture cards/word cards around for children to choose during child-initiated time.

Extend the activities

๑ Add other objects, pictures and word cards to the bag as the children become more proficient. Use more complex words, eg,

ch-ur-ch church,

sh-i-p ship,

n-igh-t night,

m-oo-n moon.

FOCUS Aspect 7 – Oral blending and segmenting

๑ Tuning into sounds (auditory discrimination)
📣 Listening and remembering (auditory memory and sequencing)
☺ Talking about sounds (developing vocabulary and language comprehension)

TALKING BAG
Tune: Jack and Jill

Talking bag, so what's inside?
We'll find a toy that's trying to hide.

Make the sounds talk, say the word,
We'll listen then we'll copy.

Child: C-a-t
All copy: C-a-t

ROBOT

Using the song

🎧 Explain the game to the children. They will hear a robot song and, at the end of the verse, they will try to work out the word the robot has said. By blending the three segmented sounds that the robot has made they will try to say the word out loud.

Play track 30 to the children or sing the song yourself in a robot-like voice!

Add robot actions with stiff arms, moving to the beat.

Child-initiated play

☺ Provide materials for the children to make a robot, or a robot costume which they can wear to play the game. Leave sets of word cards with familiar CVC words for the robot to sound out for other children to guess the words to remind the children of the list of sounds they collected.

Extend the activities

🎧 Use letter cards and show the children each letter as the robot speaks each sound. Can they identify the whole word? Can they choose the correct card to replace the first sound, eg, changing c-a-t to m-a-t?

Play the game by singing the song with other sets of CVC words, eg, pig, big, dig; pan, man, ran.

What you will need

- Materials to make a robot or robot costume for someone to wear.
- Word cards with familiar CVC words.
- Letter cards, Pgs 79–80.

FOCUS Aspect 7 – Oral blending and segmenting

🎧 Tuning into sounds (auditory discrimination)
🦻 Listening and remembering (auditory memory and sequencing)
☺ Talking about sounds (developing vocabulary and language comprehension)

ROBOT

I'm a little metal robot,
You can see me walk.
I use special sounds to make me talk.
Listen to me speaking, sounding out the word: c-a-t.
Now, can you say the word you heard? (cat)

I'm a little metal robot,
You can see me walk.
I use special sounds to make me talk.
Listen to me speaking, sounding out the word: b-a-t.
Now, can you say the word you heard? (bat)

I'm a little metal robot,
You can see me walk.
I use special sounds to make me talk.
Listen to me speaking, sounding out the word: h-a-t.
Now, can you say the word you heard? (hat)

I'm a little metal robot,
You can see me walk.
I use special sounds to make me talk.
Listen to me speaking, sounding out the word: m-a-t.
Now, can you say the word you heard? (mat)

SINGING SOUND TALK

Using the song

☺ Before listening to the song, ensure the children have an understanding of what sound talk means (see Introduction, Pg 5). Listen to track 31 and sing along with the chorus.

Show the children the object or picture card, eg, bag and show them how to sound talk b-a-g before singing the verse so that they have a firm understanding of how to separate each sound or phoneme in a word. They also need to be taught how to enunciate the phonemes correctly (see **Letters and Sounds** 00281-2007BKT-EN)

Child-initiated play

🐾 Encourage the children to play independently with the sound bag or box during child-initiated time.

Provide a toy robot for children to use when segmenting separate phonemes in words.

Extend the activities

☺ Have a few objects/picture cards in a bag or box and sound talk them as each object/card is pulled out. Follow this up by singing your own verses to match the chosen items in the bag or box.

Sound talk can also be interpreted as 'robot talk'. Children can be encouraged to separate the sounds by talking like a robot and using one robot arm movement for each individual sound: 'r-a-t' – rat.

What you will need

- Objects/picture cards for each verse, eg, bag, leg, fish and extra objects/cards for extending the activity.
- Cloth bag/box

FOCUS Aspect 7 – Oral blending and segmenting

🐾 Tuning into sounds (auditory discrimination)

🐾 Listening and remembering (auditory memory and sequencing)

☺ Talking about sounds (developing vocabulary and language comprehension)

SINGING SOUND TALK

Chorus:
We're singing a song as we sound talk,
We're singing a song to have fun,
We're singing a song as we sound talk,
So join in and play everyone.

Sound talk, sound talk,
b-a-g, b-a-g makes the word.
Sound talk, sound talk,
b-a-g, bag makes the word.

Chorus

Sound talk, sound talk,
l-e-g, l-e-g makes the word.
Sound talk, sound talk,
l-e-g, leg makes the word.

Chorus

Sound talk, sound talk,
f-i-sh, f-i-sh makes the word.
Sound talk, sound talk,
f-i-sh, fish makes the word.

CAN YOU GUESS?

Using the song

☺ Play the song on track 32 to the children encouraging them to join in with each repeating word – pot, hot and lot.

Repeat, this time sound talking each of the words: p-o-t....

When the children are confident with the song, sing it with your own choice of CVC words, eg, I'm shopping with my D-a-d.

What you will need

• A cooking pot with a wooden spoon.

• Letter or phoneme cards: p, o, t, h, l

• More letter or phoneme cards to extend the activity.

Child-initiated play

🐾 Put a cooking pot and wooden spoon along with the letter cards – p, o, t, h, l.

☺ Encourage the children to sing the song and make their own words from the letter cards by mixing them up with the spoon, then placing them in the right order at the end of each first verse.

Extend the activities

☺ Make the song more challenging by using different CVC rhyming words in each line, or by using more challenging phonemes.

We're going to see a	c-a-t,
Sitting on the	m-a-t,
We're going to see a	c-a-t,
How about	th-a-t!
We're going to see a	cat, cat, cat,
Sitting on the	mat, mat, mat,
We're going to see a	cat, cat, cat,
How about	that, that, that!

We're going to make a	w-i-sh,
That soon we'll catch a	f-i-sh,
And when we've caught the	f-i-sh,
Then we'll put it in a	d-i-sh!
We're going to make a	wish, wish, wish,
That soon we'll catch a	fish, fish, fish,
And when we've caught the	fish, fish, fish,
Then we'll put it in a	dish, dish, dish!

FOCUS Aspect 7 – Oral segmenting and blending

🎵 Tuning into sounds (auditory discrimination)

🐾 Listening and remembering (auditory memory and sequencing)

☺ Talking about sounds (developing vocabulary and language comprehension)

CAN YOU GUESS?

Tune: John Brown's body

Chorus:
Can you guess the words we're singing in this song?
Can you guess the words we're singing in this song?
Can you guess the words we're singing in this song?
When we're playing our sound talk game.

We are cooking in a p-o-t,
We are cooking in a p-o-t,
We are cooking in a p-o-t,
We're cooking in a pot, pot, pot.

Chorus

We will make it very it h-o-t,
We will make it very it h-o-t,
We will make it very it h-o-t,
We'll make it very it hot, hot, hot,

Chorus

And then we'll eat the l-o-t!
And then we'll eat the l-o-t!
And then we'll eat the l-o-t!
And then we'll eat the lot, lot, lot!

MELODY LINES

SOUNDS AROUND - Farmer's in the den

LISTENING BAG - This old man

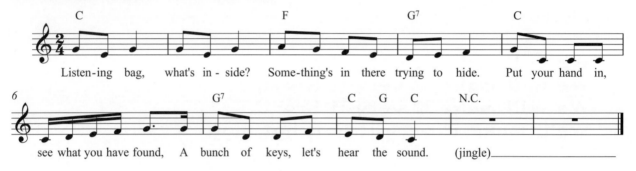

THREE SMALL PETS - Three blind mice

 SINGING PHONICS 1 © HELEN MACGREGOR & CATHERINE BIRT 2008 **A & C BLACK PUBLISHERS LTD**

HEAR, HEAR! - London's burning

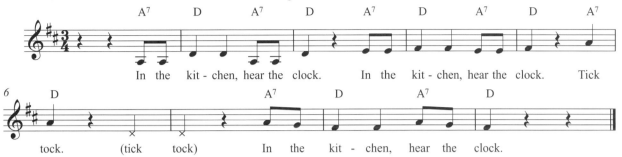

SQUEAKY DOOR - In and out the dusty bluebells

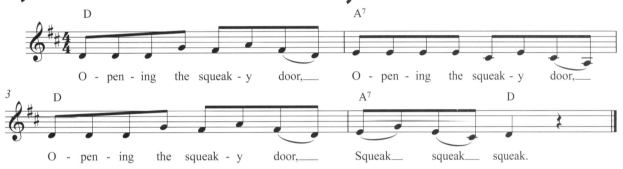

I HEAR MUSIC - Frère Jacques

READY, STEADY STOP! - London Bridge

MELODY LINES

SOUND MATCH

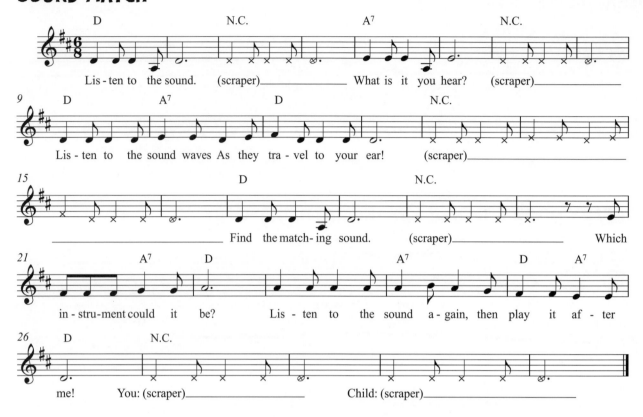

Lis-ten to the sound. (scraper)_____ What is it you hear? (scraper)_____

Lis-ten to the sound waves As they tra-vel to your ear! (scraper)_____

_____ Find the match-ing sound. (scraper)_____ Which

in-stru-ment could it be? Lis-ten to the sound a-gain, then play it af-ter

me! You: (scraper)_____ Child: (scraper)_____

INSTRUMENT PARTY

Chorus: Oh, the in-stru-ments are hav-ing a par-ty, It's in-stru-ment par-ty

time. They play and dance, they dance and play, Mak-ing mu-sic all the

night and day. Oh, the Verse: Shake, shake, shak-ing on the

shak-ers, Shak-it-y, shak-it-y, shake, shake, shake.

Shake, shake, shak-ing on the shak-ers, Shake, shake, shak-it-y shake.

SUPER SINGERS! - Pop goes the weasel

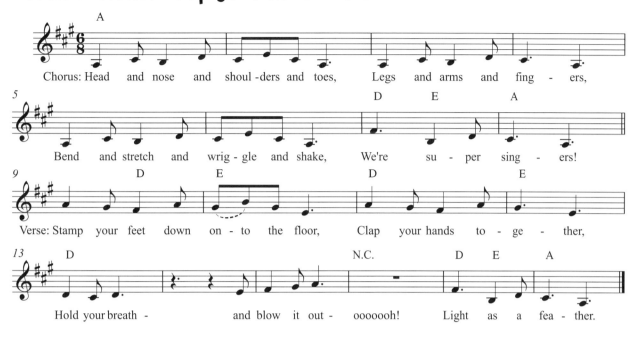

NOISY NEIGHBOURS - Skip to my lou

MELODY LINES

COPYCATS

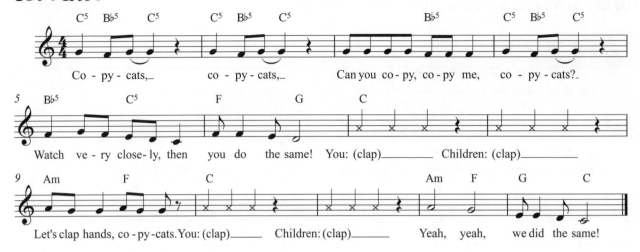

HICKORY DICKORY DONG – Hickory dickory dock

NEW PLACES – My bonnie lies over the ocean

 SINGING PHONICS 1 © HELEN MACGREGOR & CATHERINE BIRT 2008 **A & C BLACK PUBLISHERS LTD**

DAVE THE BAT

I have a lit-tle bat and he lives in a cave, He's my fur-ry friend and his name is Dave. He

hangs from the raf-ters all day long, And as he hangs he___ sings this song:

Flip flap, blink blink, squeak squeak! Flip flap, blink blink, squeak squeak!

HUBBLE BUBBLE POT

Hub-ble bub-ble hub-ble bub-ble, What's in the pot? Hub-ble bub-ble hub-ble bub-ble,

What have we got? Bug, ball, bee-tle, brush, That's what we've got in the pot!

SOCKS AND SNAKES - London Bridge

Socks and snakes and sau-sa-ges, Sau-sa-ges, sau-sa-ges,

Socks and snakes and sau-sa-ges, s s s s.

PINKY PARTY PIG - Old MacDonald

Sing the sound that starts these words: Pin-ky par-ty pig.

Sing the sound that starts these words: Pin-ky par-ty pig. With a

p p here and a p p there, Here a p, there a p, ev-'ry where a p p.

Sing the sound that starts these words: Pin-ky par-ty pig.

SOUND BOX - Here we go round the mulberry bush

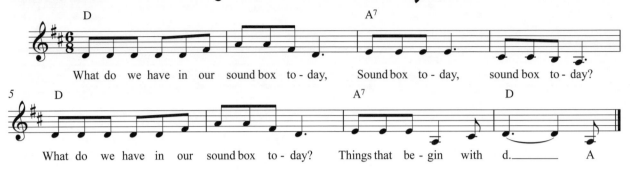

What do we have in our sound box to-day, Sound box to-day, sound box to-day?

What do we have in our sound box to-day? Things that be-gin with d._____ A

OUT TO PLAY - Jelly on a plate

Go-ing out to play, Go-ing out to play.

Hoo-ray, hoo-ray, hoo-ray, hoo-ray! Go-ing out to play.

PROFESSOR BRAIN'S AMAZING MACHINE

Pro-fess-or Brain built a great ma-chine Made out of me-tal and

tin. It can do a-ny-thing that you ask it to, Just press the but-tons

in, And it goes... Whirr, whirr, click, click, whirr, whirr,

click, click. It's the most_____ a-ma-zing ma-chine!

SINGALONGA NOAH

CAN YOU MAKE THE SOUNDS? - The wheels on the bus

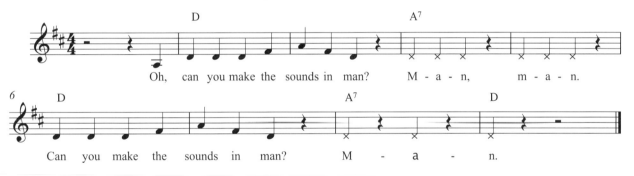

TALKING BAG

ROBOT

I'm a lit-tle me-tal ro-bot, You can see me walk. I use spe-cial sounds to make me talk.

Lis-ten to me speak-ing, sound-ing out the word: c - a - t. Now, can you say the word you heard? (cat)

SINGING SOUND TALK

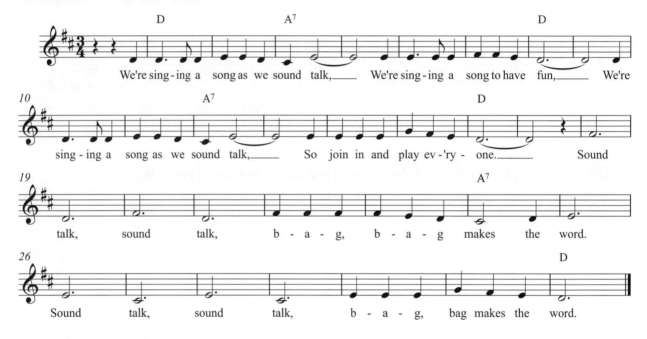

We're sing-ing a song as we sound talk,___ We're sing-ing a song to have fun,___ We're

sing-ing a song as we sound talk,___ So join in and play ev-'ry-one.___ Sound

talk, sound talk, b - a - g, b - a - g makes the word.

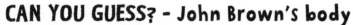

Sound talk, sound talk, b - a - g, bag makes the word.

CAN YOU GUESS? - John Brown's body

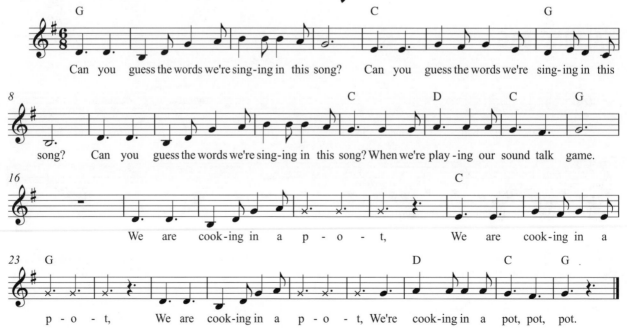

Can you guess the words we're sing-ing in this song? Can you guess the words we're sing-ing in this

song? Can you guess the words we're sing-ing in this song? When we're play-ing our sound talk game.

We are cook-ing in a p - o - t, We are cook-ing in a

p - o - t, We are cook-ing in a p - o - t, We're cook-ing in a pot, pot, pot.

 SINGING PHONICS 1 © HELEN MACGREGOR & CATHERINE BIRT 2008 A & C BLACK PUBLISHERS LTD

a b c d

e f g h

i j k l

m n o p

q r s t

u v w x

y z

SINGING PHONICS 1 © HELEN MACGREGOR & CATHERINE BIRT 2008 **A & C BLACK PUBLISHERS LTD**